The Blue Bird's Palace

written by Orianne Lallemand
illustrated by Carole Hénaff
translated by Tessa Strickland

Barefoot Books
step inside a story

On a still summer night, when the stars in the sky blazed so brightly that all the flowers stayed awake just to gaze at them, a baby girl was born.

It was harvest time in the Blue Forest. The baby's father, Nikolai, was busy day and night in the family orchard. At this time of year, folk came from far and wide to buy fruit from him, or to purchase the spiced bread and sweet jams made by his wife, Anna.

Nikolai heard the news of his baby's arrival from a radiant blue bird. He hurried home as fast as he could, and he was met by a sight even more beautiful than the stars in the night sky. The baby girl was a miracle. They named her Natasha.

Life was good.

As she grew up, little Natasha would often help her
parents in the orchard. She liked to climb the ladders
to the tallest branches of the fruit trees, pick the
very best apples and fill up the fruit baskets.
If she felt tired, she would curl up like a cat
under the trees and fall asleep.

Natasha was only seven years old when an ice-cold winter gripped the Blue Forest. Her mother, Anna, fell gravely ill. Nikolai was desperate. He called the best doctors he could find to restore his wife's health, but there was nothing anyone could do.

Winter left at last — and it carried Anna away. All the joy that had once filled the household left with her.

The death of his beloved wife broke Nikolai. He hid his tears so that he could comfort Natasha. Then, as soon as spring returned, he busied himself with work.

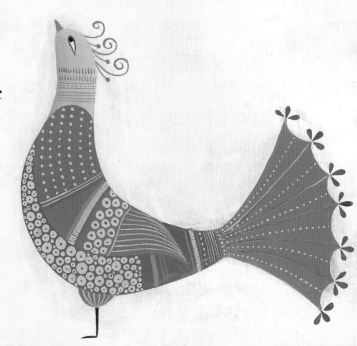

Time passed, and Natasha grew up to become a fine young woman. She was so like her mother! Nikolai could not help but adore her. Only the tastiest food was good enough for his dear daughter; only the sweetest fruits and the finest fabrics and, of course, only the best stories.

By the time she was sixteen, Natasha was truly beautiful. But she could change as suddenly as the weather — sweet as sunshine if she got her own way, savage as a storm if she did not. Whenever she was bored, she wanted something new — new clothes, a new bedroom, another songbird . . .

One morning, Natasha told her father that it was time to move. She needed a bigger, better house. But Nikolai loved his cottage. For once, he stood firm.

Natasha screamed. Natasha sobbed. Natasha shouted. Natasha stomped her feet. Nothing worked. In a towering rage, she swept out of the cottage and into the forest. She was so consumed by her own fury that she barely noticed the old woman who was coming along the path.

"Good morning, my child," said the strange old woman. "I see you have some tasty fruit in your basket. May I take one?"

"Oh very well — but just one," said Natasha grumpily. "I don't suppose you have any money to pay for it."

The old woman's eyes blazed, but she said sweetly, "I'd like to take an apple, and although I have no money, I shall grant you one wish to repay you for your kindness."

The old woman raised her right arm and a radiant blue bird, a bird more exquisite than any Natasha had ever set her eyes upon, came to perch on her wrist.

The bird held Natasha's gaze in his golden eyes and sang to her:

"Behold the guardian of the Blue Forest!
 Her power is boundless, her wisdom too.
 Make your wish with care;
 Let your heart be pure and true."

The old woman settled down on a tree stump and started munching her apple.

Natasha wondered what she should wish for. This was her chance!

"I'd like a palace!" she announced. "Not just any old palace, though, a magical one — one where I can invent all kinds of different rooms whenever I like."

The old woman sighed. She had secretly watched Natasha growing up, and she had seen her heart growing ever harder. It was high time this girl learned a lesson.

"Your wish will be granted," she said, "but on one condition. You will not be able to leave this magical palace."

"That's quite
all right,"
said Natasha.
"I won't want to."

At this, the old woman raised
her arms. There was a flash
of blue lightning, a whirl of
feathers, the sweet song of a
bird and, somewhere far off, the
sound of someone weeping.

Then everything vanished —
the old woman, the bird
and Natasha.

When Natasha woke up much, much later, she found herself all alone in a magnificent red sitting room. In the middle of the room, there were two armchairs and a small table. Exquisite blue flowers wove patterns across the walls and the tablecloth. Their workmanship was so fine that the flowers almost looked as if they were real.

Natasha dared herself to touch them. Then she looked around. There was something strange about this room. That was it! There was no door.

Natasha was amazed. Her wish had been granted! Here she was, in the palace of her dreams. And she could design it just the way she wanted, one room at a time.

She closed her eyes, eager to test her power. First, she imagined a bedroom for herself. It would be utterly luxurious, with a splendid double bed, the finest white sheets, and a mattress as soft as swan's down. She would have a wardrobe full of dresses, all of them made from the most sumptuous fabrics: taffeta, silk and velvet.

Natasha finished her wish and half opened her eyes. A door had appeared in the wall of the red sitting room, and when she opened it, she saw everything she had just wished for! She was beside herself with delight.

She threw herself onto the bed — and instantly fell asleep.

When she awoke the
next day, Natasha was ravenous.
She wasted no time. First, she wished
for an enormous kitchen. Then she wished
for all of the foods she loved most: golden
freshly baked bread, cheeses, bowls of fruit
and all kinds of delicacies that she had only
heard about but never tasted.

When she had eaten her fill, she set about
designing a garden that would remind her
of the forest where she had spent her childhood.
Enormous fruit trees sprang up, each one more
beautiful than the last. Wild flowers carpeted the
ground, and there was even a babbling brook for
her to paddle in.

Natasha sighed with pleasure. She did not notice
that no birds sang in her garden. She did not notice
that no breeze murmured in the leaves of the trees.

Day after day, Natasha dreamed up new rooms
for herself. Before long, it took her an entire day
to walk from one end of her palace to the other.

One morning, Natasha woke up with a heavy heart. She pecked restlessly at her breakfast. Then she went to the window of the red sitting room. This was the only window that looked out onto the world.

Far away, Natasha could see an orchard. Its trees were covered with apples; the sun was shining on them.

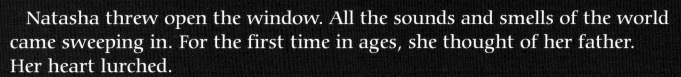

Natasha threw open the window. All the sounds and smells of the world came sweeping in. For the first time in ages, she thought of her father. Her heart lurched.

What was he doing now? Did he miss her? What if he had died of grief?

Natasha slammed the window shut.

At once, she felt herself being pulled back. The blue flowers on the wall and the tablecloth had come to life, and their long stems were winding themselves around her. One seized her hair, another her waist, another her shoulders, her wrist . . . Soon, she was completely entangled. She fell to the ground, senseless.

When Natasha awoke, she was in utter darkness.
She lay on the floor and sobbed. If only the guardian
of the forest would return; she would tell her
how much she regretted her actions . . .

Thanks to her wish, she had made
herself her own prisoner. She tried to sit up,
only to discover that her arms had turned into wings. Her feet had
become claws, her mouth was now a beak, and her body was covered
with long, silky feathers.

She had become a blue bird.

Once more, she felt herself drawn to the outside world. She spread her wings wide and flew. This time, the blue flowers did not pull her back.

It was extraordinary to fly! Oh, it was wonderful! All of Natasha's troubles fell away. From the sky, her palace looked just like an ordinary cottage. Fields and villages stretched out beneath her as far as the eye could see.

Throughout that night, Natasha flew around her domain. She saw families huddled together in cottages with just one room. She heard the cries of hungry children. She understood what it meant to be poor. She understood what it meant to live in hardship.

At sunrise, she flew back to her palace with a heavy heart. As soon as she had crossed the windowsill, she returned to her human form. But deep inside, she had changed.

Natasha found the simple dress that she had
been wearing when she first imagined her palace.
There would be no more dressing-up sessions; no
more walks through her splendid rooms; no more
magnificent feasts . . . One by one, the rooms
disappeared. Soon, only the sitting room, the
kitchen, the bedroom and the garden remained.

Natasha spent her time quite differently now.
Every day, she gathered fruit in the garden.
Then she made jams and baked loaves of spiced
bread. Little by little, she started to remember her
childhood. Little by little, her heart softened and
began to open.

Every night, Natasha turned herself into a blue
bird and flew out of the palace. She took with her
baskets of the bread she had made during the day
and left loaves on the doorsteps of the poorest
cottages she could find.

And everyone blessed these gifts that fell at night
from the sky.

One evening, Natasha was resting in the red sitting room when she noticed a blue bird on the windowsill. The bird sang a song so sad and so tender that tears started streaming down Natasha's cheeks. She felt like a little girl again, running to greet her father when he came in from work. She felt the warmth of her mother's arms around her shoulders.

When at last the song came to an end, the old woman was sitting opposite her.

"Good evening," said Natasha politely. "I am so happy to see you again."

"And I am happy to see you, Natasha," the old woman replied. "I am also happy to see that your heart has opened. It is time for you to go home now."

Once more, the old woman raised her arms. Once more, there was a flash of blue lightning, a whirl of feathers, the sweet song of a bird and somewhere, far off, the sound of someone laughing.

Then everything vanished — the old woman, the bird, the red sitting room and Natasha.

Natasha opened her eyes. She was lying in the grass at the heart of the Blue Forest. It was a still summer night. The stars in the sky blazed so brightly that all the flowers stayed awake just to gaze at them.

Slowly and carefully, Natasha sat up. "This is our orchard," she thought. "And this is the path that will lead me back to the cottage, and back to my dear father."

She started walking.

In the heart of the forest,
a blue bird sang.

For Solange, my fairy godmother, a story to share with the little ones — O. L.

For Anouk, Nina and Noah — C. H.

Barefoot Books
2067 Massachusetts Ave
Cambridge, MA 02140

Barefoot Books
29/30 Fitzroy Square
London, W1T 6LQ

Text by Orianne Lallemand
Illustrations by Carole Hénaff
First published in France as *Le Palais de l'Oiseau Bleu*
© Hachette Livre / Gautier-Languereau, 2011
Translation copyright © 2016 by Tessa Strickland
The moral rights of Orianne Lallemand and Carole Hénaff have been asserted

First published in Great Britain by Barefoot Books, Ltd
and in the United States of America by Barefoot Books, Inc in 2016
This paperback edition first published in 2019
All rights reserved

Graphic design by Sarah Soldano, Barefoot Books
Reproduction by B & P International, Hong Kong
Printed in China on 100% acid-free paper
This book was typeset in Caleigh and Carmina Md
The illustrations were prepared in acrylics

Hardback ISBN 978-1-84686-885-6
Paperback ISBN 978-1-78285-911-6

British Cataloguing-in-Publication Data:
a catalogue record for this book is available from the British Library

Library of Congress Cataloging-in-Publication Data
is available under LCCN 2016039294

3 5 7 9 8 6 4 2